A Window of Time

NADJA Publishing

Special Thanks to John Huff

Text Copyright © 1995 by Audrey Leighton
Illustration Copyright © 1995 by Rhonda Kyrias
Editorial Maria McNeill

NADJA Publishing
P.O. Box 326, Lake Forest, CA 92630

NADJA Publishing
Jennifer Brooks
P.O. Box 326
Lake Forest, CA 92630
714/459-9750
Fax: 714/858-3477

Library of Congress Cataloging-in-Publication Data

Leighton, Audrey O.
    A window of time / written by Audrey O. Leighton, illustrated by
Rhonda Kyrias.
    p. cm.
    ISBN 0-9636335-1-1

    1. Alzheimer's disease—Juvenile fiction. 2. Aged—Juvenile
fiction. 3. Grandparents—Juvenile fiction.   I. Title.

PZ7.L454Wind 1995   [Fic]
                                                     QBI95-20017

Preassigned LCCN: 95-067526

Printed in Hong Kong
10 9 8 7 6 5 4 3 2 1

In memory of my father,
Arthur Edward Olson
and to George, a friend forever.
With love for Bob.
A.L.

To Dorothy
R.K.

*G*randpa has a secret time machine
that takes him back to when he was young.

Back to when he lived on a farm.

Back to when he played with Jack.

Sometimes Grandpa calls me Jack. I am not Jack.
I am Shawn. Jack was Grandpa's younger brother.

Grandpa says, "Come, Jack, we need to bring the cows to milk. When we find the cows in the meadow, I will put you on Bess for a ride."

My grandpa has no cows.
My grandpa lives in the city.

But I would like to ride on Bess.

Once when my grandpa and I cut up seed potatoes, he said,
"I would like a cool drink of water from the well my father dug.
When Father dug our well, my mother pulled the dirt up in a bucket.
We all helped to pull him up when water filled the well."

My grandpa has no well.
I bring him a glass of water from the faucet in our kitchen.

When Grandpa and I go down to the pond,
my mother gives us a sack of bread to feed the ducks.
"Shawn," she says, "do not push Grandpa too fast."

But Grandpa says, "Go fast so I can feel the wind on my face.
Just like when I rode on Star."
"Who was Star, Grandpa?" I ask.
"Star was our horse. She pulled our threshing machine. After work I
rode her back to the barn. She ran so fast to get her oats, I felt the
wind on my face."

I whinny like a horse and push my grandpa as fast as the wind. Grandpa laughs and says, "That's more like it. Giddy up, Shawn!"

There are times my grandpa calls me Jack.

There are times my grandpa calls me Shawn.

There are times my grandpa thinks
he lives on a farm.

There are times my grandpa remembers
he lives in the city.

There are times my grandpa forgets what he did in the morning.
But he remembers what he did sixty-five years ago.

My grandpa says that memories are like a window of time.

Through Grandpa's window I can see his life as a boy, long before I was born.

When Grandpa gets mixed up, my mother tells him,
"Dad, your time machine is on the fritz again."

Grandpa says, "Well, well, is it now?"

Then Grandpa winks at me.

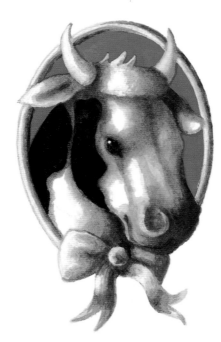